IF DINOSAURS HAD HAIR

Dan Marvin

Illustrated by **Lesley Vamos**

Roaring Brook Press
New York

Could you imagine if dinosaurs had . . .

Why, if dinosaurs had hair,
they must have had parents who
brushed it too hard.

And siblings who pulled it.

And snarls.

SO.

MANY.

SNARLS.

If dinosaurs had hair . . .

. . . they probably liked to show it off.

Flying with flair.

Galloping with gusto.

Swimming with sass.

Some probably checked
their reflections a lot.

Like, A LOT.

And all that drama
and sass and gossip . . .

Pompadour-o-saurus was a trendsetting T. rex.

Hair-o-dactyl was a pterodactyl with taste.

Team Hair-o-dactyl hollered,
"The styles are wild and so are we!"

Team Pompadour-o-saurus yelled,
"It's Jurassic and we look fantastic!"

A woolly mammoth said,
"I think I'm early. But how's my hair?"

Why, if dinosaurs had hair, the hair wars would get wild.

From pigtails to pixie cuts . . .

. . . from pageboys to perms.

From bowl cuts to brush cuts
to bouffants and braids.

From mod cuts to mop tops
to flattops and fades.

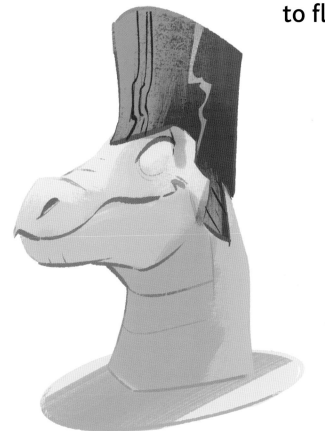

Eventually, one style would
rise above them all.

Literally . . .

If dinosaurs had hair . . .

. . . that may be the reason
they're no longer here.

For Denny Marvin, who I
inHAIRited the dad joke gene from
—D.M.

For Ash, for letting me play with all your dinosaurs,
and for his little brother, who cheered me on from the inside :)

—L.V.

Published by Roaring Brook Press
Roaring Brook Press is a division of Holtzbrinck Publishing Holdings Limited Partnership
120 Broadway, New York, NY 10271 • mackids.com

Text copyright © 2022 by Dan Marvin
Illustrations copyright © 2022 by Lesley Vamos
All rights reserved.

Library of Congress Cataloging-in-Publication Data is available.
ISBN 978-1-250-79256-3

Our books may be purchased in bulk for promotional, educational, or business use.
Please contact your local bookseller or the Macmillan Corporate and Premium Sales Department
at (800) 221-7945 ext. 5442 or by email at MacmillanSpecialMarkets@macmillan.com.

First edition, 2022

The illustrations for this book were created using Adobe Photoshop.
This book was edited by Mekisha Telfer and Connie Hsu. It was designed by Cindy De la Cruz and Mariam Quraishi.
The production editors were Taylor Pitts and Kat Kopit, and the production manager was Susan Doran.

Printed in China by Toppan Leefung Printing Ltd., Dongguan City, Guangdong Province

1 3 5 7 9 10 8 6 4 2